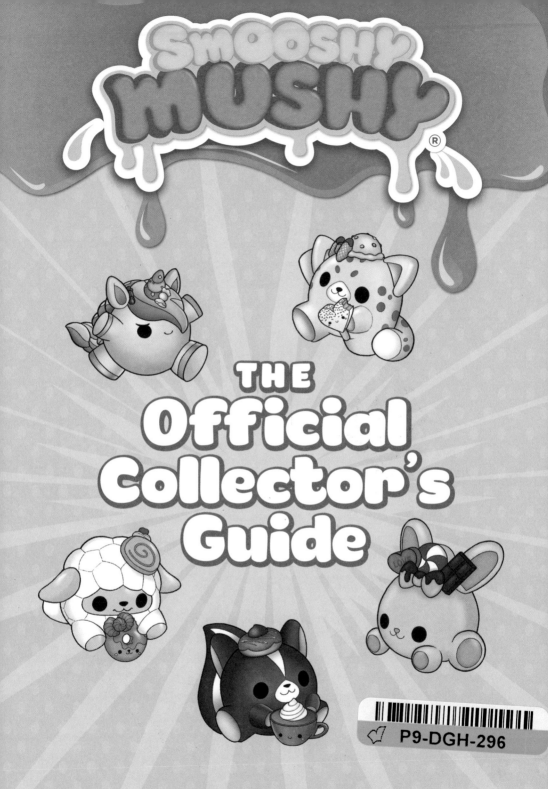

SMOOSHY MUSHY®

THE Official Collector's Guide

BuzzPop

P9-DGH-296

BuzzPop

An imprint of Bonnier Publishing USA
251 Park Avenue South, New York, NY 10010
Copyright TM and © 2019 OLO Industries, LLC
All rights reserved, including the right of reproduction
in whole or in part in any form.
BuzzPop is a trademark of Bonnier Publishing USA, and associated
colophon is a trademark of Bonnier Publishing USA.

Manufactured in the United States of America LAK 1218
First Edition

1 3 5 7 9 10 8 6 4 2

ISBN 978-1-4998-0961-9

buzzpopbooks.com
bonnierpublishingusa.com

Welcome, Smooshy Squad!

You have found the ultimate source of information on the sweet-smelling and oh, so squishy inhabitants of Smooshyville. Here, you can discover never-before-known facts and get to know these mysterious and mischievous creatures.

With so many characters to collect, it's hard to keep track of them all. But now with this book, you've got *all* the latest Smooshys from series 1-5 in your hands. Check off the characters you already have. So grab your Besties and dive in!

The Legend of Smooshyville

During the day, the town of Smooshyville is a lot like other towns, maybe even yours. There are people, cars, hustle and bustle. When the town goes to sleep, however, the pets from the local animal shelter sneak out with mischief on their minds. No one knows how or when it started, but these adorable little tricksters have been finding trouble for quite a while now. Of course, sometimes trouble finds them.

Their favorite hangout is a food factory called Smooshy Mushy Industries. It's here that some squishy treats fill their tummies, while others have filled their hearts! That's right—certain special food items have become Besties with the Smooshies. From donuts to pancakes to French fries, the fabulous, foodilicious friends are always ready to share a smile or an adventure. And maybe most importantly, they help Smooshies get out of some pretty sticky situations.

Find Your Smooshy Mushy Name!

1st Letter of Your First Name	1st Letter of Your Last Name
A – Squishy	A – Crumbs
B – Happy	B – Berry
C – Fluffy	C – Whiskers
D – Mushy	D – Fritter
E – Adorable	E – Marshmallow
F – Giggles	F – Biscuit
G – Sugary	G – Cupcake
H – Nutty	H – Burger
I – Smooshy	I – Lollipop
J – Honey	J – Choco-Latte
K – Sticky	K – Bubbles
L – Fruity	L – Noodle
M – Gooey	M – Churro
N – Spicy	N – Sugar Cake
O – Crunchy	O – Sprinkles
P – Sassy	P – Cutie Pie
Q – Cuddly	Q – Twinkle Toes
R – Swooshy	R – Snuggles
S – Cutie	S – Puddin' Pop
T – Lucky	T – Jelly Bean
U – Shimmer	U – Lamb Chop
V – Tangy	V – Pickle
W – Silly	W – Candy Pop
X – Yummy	X – Sweet Toot
Y – Shiny	Y – Peep
Z – Messy	Z – Lovebug

A Day in Smooshyville

Fill in the blanks below, then read the story to discover what would happen to you in Smooshyville.

This morning, I put on my _____ _____
favorite food item of clothing

and went to meet my friend, _____
texture flavor

_____, at the Sunny Side Cafe. When I arrived
food item

and met my friend, Charlita Chicky told us it was closed due to

a _____ overflow. My friend and I were supposed
beverage

to be writing our new hit _____ called
type of entertainment

_____ _____ _____.
type of fruit something soft profession

Instead, we decided to help Charlita with the mess.

Thankfully, my friend and I both always carry an extra

_____ for emergencies. We used them to
something made out of cloth

help Charlita clean up. Before we knew it, the cafe was open and

bustling. Bitsy Bunny was busy with her _____
something sweet

donut, and Suki Squirrel was sipping her _____
flavor

-oh's and milk. Charlita even thought of a new special

dessert, overflowing, three-friend _____.
type of pastry

It was _____ ! My friend and I got a great
adjective

idea for another project, the _____
adjective

_____ Helpers!
a meal

6

Smooshy Pets!

Find out who is hiding in the Blind Packs!

Series 1-5

Bitsy Bunny

A little clumsy, but this bun is ready for fun!

Favorite Dance: the bunny hop
Always: lands frosting-side up!
Personal Quote: Ear-ly to bed, ear-ly to rise!
Hides in: chocolate milkshakes
Bestie: Dani Donut

○

This paw-sitive bear can find the
funny in any situation.

Biggest Fear: laughing her tail off
Best at: bear hugs!
Personal Quote: It's waff-ly nice to meet you!
Hides in: maple syrup
Bestie: Barley Bacon

○

Messy adventures are fine
with this swine!

Can Be Found: snout and about
Secret Skill: banking
Personal Quote: Butter late than never!
Hides in: maple syrup
Bestie: Punkin Pancake

Felina Fawn

With more than cupcakes on the brain,
she can think her way out of trouble.

Reads: hoof-done-it mysteries
Sweet Skill: doe-ting on friends
Personal Quote: I do what I dear!
Hides in: chocolate milkshakes
Bestie: Chessie Chocolate

Lolli Lamb

A little sheepish, but fun for the whole flock!

Enjoys: the baaa-soo
Sweet Skill: counting
Personal Quote: Wool you be mine?
Hides in: chocolate milkshakes
Bestie: Cami Cotton Candy

Kaley Kitty

This crafty ringleader never takes a paws.

Looks Forward to: Caturdays
Sweet Skill: purr-fect planning
Personal Quote: Hear meow-t!
Hides in: tomato ketchup
Bestie: Mooky Milk

FRANKIE FRENCHY

A little bit salty, but she's sweet on adventure.

Obsession: bur-grrrrrs
Vacation Activity: the running of the bulldogs
Personal Quote: Don't wait pup!
Hides in: tomato ketchup
Bestie: Fritzy Frie

Suki Squirrel

She rarely looks before she leaps or even needs to.

Favorite Ballet: *The Nutcracker*
Favorite TV Show: *Gossip Squirrel*
Personal Quote: All my friends are a little nutty.
Hides in: tomato ketchup
Bestie: Nimi Nut

◯ Chalsea Chick

Mischief is always in style with this posh pet!

Would Drive a: coop
Sweet Skill: winging it
Personal Quote: Birds of a feather are
ready for adventure!
Hides in: cotton candy milk
Bestie: Sophie Strawberry

○ Sammi Skunk

Always there when you need her,
you can tell by the smell!

Favorite Letters: P & U
Aspires to Be: a zebra
Personal Quote: If you can't stand the smell,
get out of the kitchen!
Hides in: strawberry milk
Bestie: Choco Mint

○ Lauren Lambie

Enjoys adventures with a softer side.

Biggest Fear: not having the chops
Favorite Celebrity: Mary's little lamb
Personal Quote: Maybe we should
turn baaa-ck.
Hides in: cotton candy milk
Bestie: Billie Bun

○Vanessa Vanilla

She has refined tastes, and a great sense of smell!

Hangs Around: the groomers
Shops at: pup-up stores
Personal Quote: Don't poo-poodle it until you've tried it!
Hides in: raspberry milk
Bestie: Milkwhite

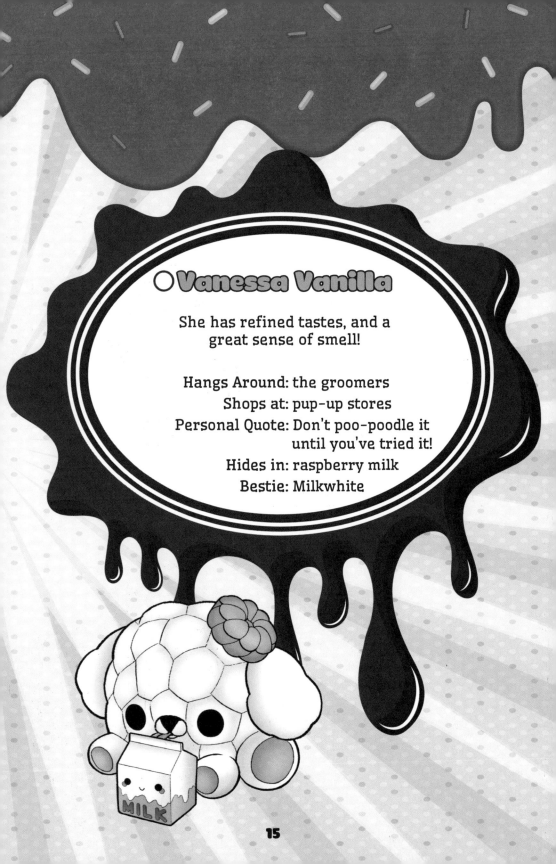

◯ Casey Cow

Always looking out for everyone
else, she's a real pal!

Biggest Fear: being a cow-herd
Sweet Skill: moon jumping
Personal Quote: It's pasture bedtime.
Hides in: strawberry milk
Bestie: Sunnyside

◯ Mackenzie Monkey

Always the artist, each of her adventures
has a creative flair.

Fears: jumping on the bed
Loves: hanging out
Personal Quote: I see, I do.
Hides in: raspberry milk
Bestie: Pierre Croissant

do-dat donuts

○ Labella Lamb

She loves to share everything
from adventures to snuggles.

Biggest Fear: running out of fabric softener
Favorite Movie: *While You Were Sheeping*
Personal Quote: I'm more than just a
pretty fleece.
Hides in: chocolate milk
Bestie: Dita Donut

○ Cari Cow

A bit silly, she's known for her
hay-brained schemes.

Desperately Misses: the dish and the spoon
Aspires to Be: in the moo-vies
Personal Quote: That's udder-ly ridiculous!
Hides in: strawberry milk
Bestie: Mitzi Milk

○ Petula Poodle

A total smarty, she can lick any problem!

Favorite Song: "Don't Be Crull"
Role Model: Joan of Bark
Personal Quote: That deserves a
round of a-paws!
Hides in: chocolate milk
Bestie: Casey Croissant

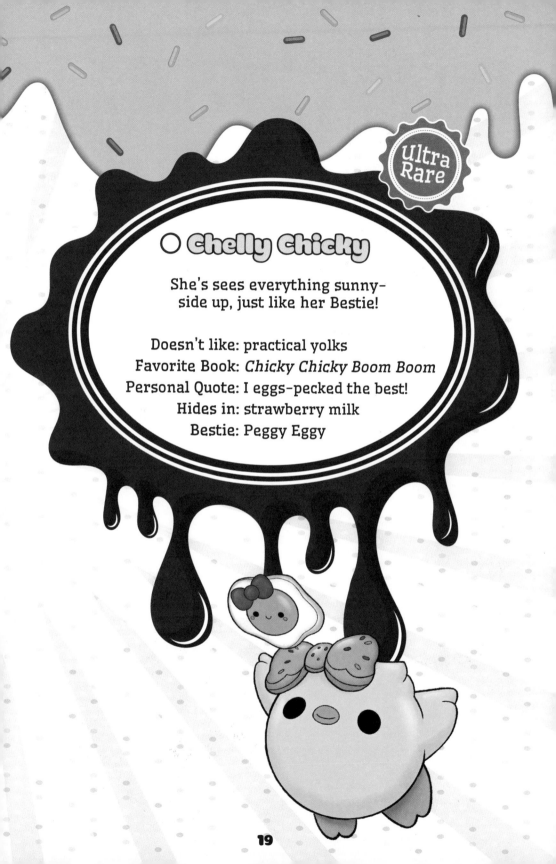

○ Chelly Chicky

She's sees everything sunnyside up, just like her Bestie!

Doesn't like: practical yolks
Favorite Book: *Chicky Chicky Boom Boom*
Personal Quote: I eggs-pecked the best!
Hides in: strawberry milk
Bestie: Peggy Eggy

Ultra
Rare

○ Marney Monkey

Calm and collected, she's prime
mate for any scheme.

Often Found in: barrels
Works out at: the jungle gym
Personal Quote: That's bananas!
Hides in: vanilla milk
Bestie: Cora Cocoa

○ Kaila Koala

Stubborn, but determined, she
eventually gets what she's after!

Listens to: Eu-calypso
Often Found: down under
Personal Quote: Be-claws I said so!
Hides in: strawberry milk
Bestie: Charla Chocolate Milk

○ Scout Skunk

She's a little explorer with classic style.

Dislikes: stinky cheeses
Listens to: skunk rock
Personal Quote: Stripes are in. They're always in.
Hides in: vanilla milk
Bestie: Cilia Cinnamon Bun

○ Bayla Bear

This party animal is the hostess with the mostest!

Never: bears her teeth
Favorite Celebrity: Goldilocks
Personal Quote: You can catch more flies with honey!
Hides in: chocolate milk
Bestie: Cala Cake

Creamery

○ Rose Rabbit

This bun-dle of energy loves to bounce, bop, and twirl all around town.

Reads: hare-raising tales
Obsessed with: bouncy castles
Personal Quote: Be there in the twitch of a nose!
Hides in: mint ice cream
Bestie: Sara Sundae

⭕ Lola Leopard

Adorable to the core, there's no stopping this stunner when she sees something she likes.

Personal Quote: I can't change my spots!
Hides in: strawberry ice cream
Bestie: Mikki Mochi

⭕ Faye Froggy

She's always ready to spring into action.

Personal Quote: Let's hop to it!
Hides in: strawberry ice cream
Bestie: Wendy Wafer

Peggy Penguin

She's chiller than ice cream, but just as sweet.

Secret Skill: pancake making—she's a great flipper!
Biggest Fear: flying
Personal Quote: It's cool!
Hides in: blueberry ice cream
Bestie: Sunny Sundae

○ Colby Corgi

Like her sister, Casey, she always has a sweet surprise for her friends.

Personal Quote: Five-second drool!
Hides in: mixed-berry ice cream
Bestie: Chilla Vanilla

○ Casey Corgi

Not to be outdone by Colby, she brings treats with a twist!

Personal Quote: Hey, corgeous!
Hides in: strawberry ice cream
Bestie: Sandy Sandwich

Mimi Monkey

A natural leader, she brings
out the best in everyone.

Personal Quote: Never stop climbing!
Hides in: mixed-berry ice cream
Bestie: Robyn Rainbow

Ultra
Rare

Suzy Snow Leopard

She's hard to spot, but she's always
there when you need her.

Personal Quote: These paws were
made for pouncin'!
Hides in: blueberry ice cream
Bestie: Bobbi Bubblegum

⭕ Aubrey Owl

This smart bird is owl-ways there for her friends.

Personal Quote: This'll be a hoot!
Hides in: purple cup
Bestie: Bethy Blueberry Pie

○ Marla Mouse

This little schemer plans down
to the very last detail.

Personal Quote: Mice think twice!
Hides in: purple cup
Bestie: Pita Petit

○ Molly Mare

Maybe the friendliest of the bunch,
she's everyone's biggest fan.

Personal Quote: Hi, there, neigh-bor!
Hides in: pink cup
Bestie: Sara Sprinklepop

○ Peyton Pony

Like her cousin, Molly, she wants to
be your bud, but she's a little shy.

Personal Quote: Want to go for a gal-pal-op?
Hides in: purple cup
Bestie: Cherry Yummins

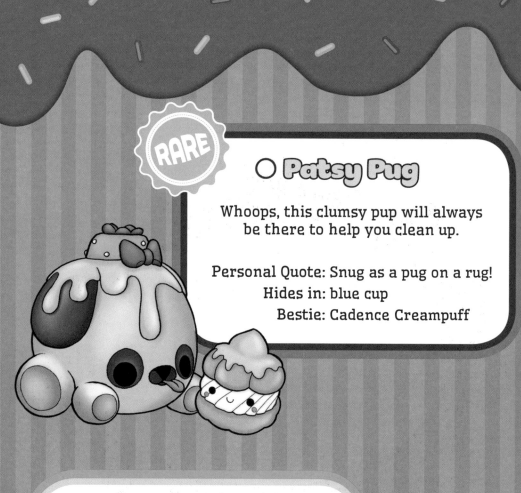

○ Patsy Pug

Whoops, this clumsy pup will always be there to help you clean up.

Personal Quote: Snug as a pug on a rug!
Hides in: blue cup
Bestie: Cadence Creampuff

○ Sailor Squeaks

Very determined, this mouse will brave anything to help her friends!

Personal Quote: Anchors a-weigh a lot more than me!
Hides in: pink cup
Bestie: Rosie Raspberry Pie

⭕ Tabby Tiger

She's a bit of a purr-fectionist, but always forgives her friends' er-roars.

Personal Quote: I make mistakes every meow and then.
Hides in: blue cup
Bestie: Fauna Fondant

⭕ Tillie Tiger

Variety is the spice of life, so she never does the same thing twice!

Personal Quote: I'd rather roar than be a bore.
Hides in: pastel pink cup
Bestie: Petunia Puff

◯ Hayley Hedgehog

She faces problems head-on and never hides from anything.

Personal Quote: Someone named a comet after me!

Hides in: gumball machine

Bestie: Libbie Lolli

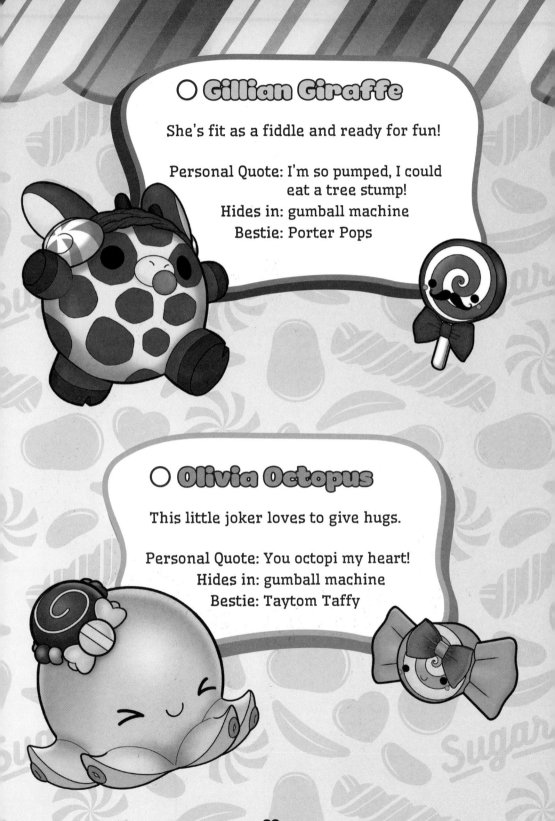

○ Gillian Giraffe

She's fit as a fiddle and ready for fun!

Personal Quote: I'm so pumped, I could eat a tree stump!
Hides in: gumball machine
Bestie: Porter Pops

○ Olivia Octopus

This little joker loves to give hugs.

Personal Quote: You octopi my heart!
Hides in: gumball machine
Bestie: Taytom Taffy

○ Selina Seal

With a splashy personality,
she's always ready to play.

Favorite Song: "Signed, Sealed, Delivered"
Personal Quote: We arf the champions!
Hides in: gumball machine
Bestie: Casey Cornball

○ Bitsy Bunny

A core Smooshy, she
just keeps bouncing back
with more sweets to share!

Personal Quote: Every day is
Bunday Funday!
Hides in: gumball machine
Bestie: Tiffy Taffy

○ Belinda Bat

RARE

Glow in the Dark

Stylish and sweet,
she's queen of the night!

Personal Quote: Is there an echo
in here?
Hides in: gumball machine
Bestie: Dottie Delish

○ Felina Fawn

This deer friend is another core Smooshy with a sweet tooth.

Personal Quote: Hoof said you can't have your cake and eat it, too?
Hides in: gumball machine
Bestie: Gracie Gum

○ Uma Unicorn

A stylish smarty, she always gets straight to the point.

Personal Quote: Lookin' sharp!
Hides in: pastel pink cup
Bestie: Flossy Fluff

Exclusive Pets!

Discover which pets can only be found in Frozen Delights!
Series 1-3
Plus, find the super-sneaky pets only found in play sets.

frozen delights

Hiding in a smoothie near you!

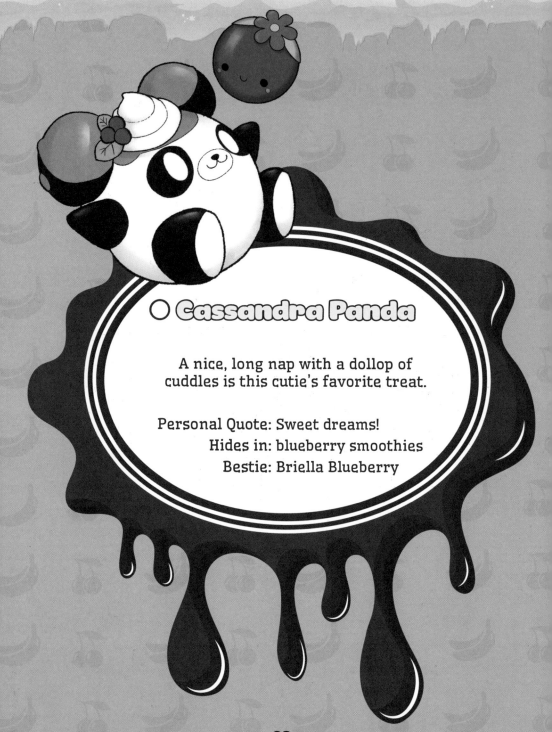

○ Cassandra Panda

A nice, long nap with a dollop of cuddles is this cutie's favorite treat.

Personal Quote: Sweet dreams!
Hides in: blueberry smoothies
Bestie: Briella Blueberry

○ Halle Hamster

She's busy, busy, but always
has time for her friends.

Personal Quote: I can't help hamming it up!
Hides in: mango lassis
Bestie: Marni Mango

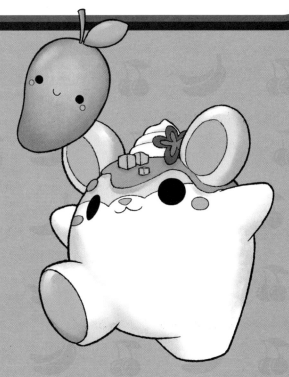

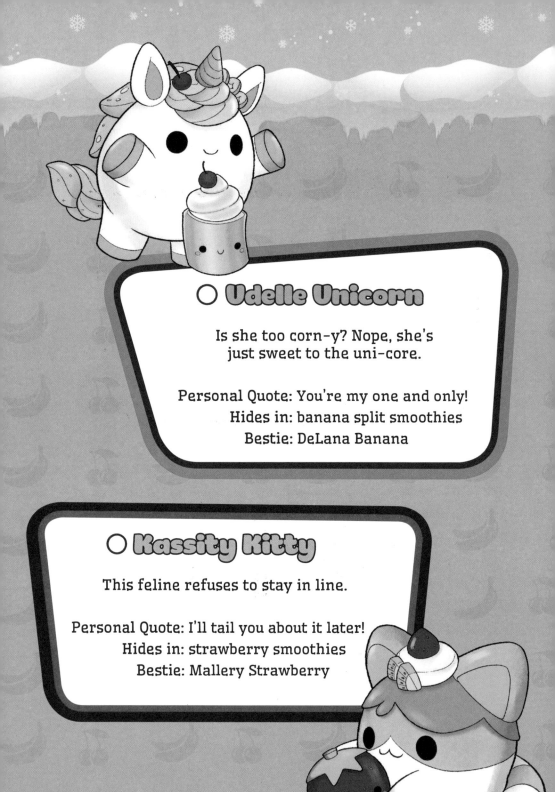

○ Udelle Unicorn

Is she too corn-y? Nope, she's
just sweet to the uni-core.

Personal Quote: You're my one and only!
Hides in: banana split smoothies
Bestie: DeLana Banana

○ Kassity Kitty

This feline refuses to stay in line.

Personal Quote: I'll tail you about it later!
Hides in: strawberry smoothies
Bestie: Mallery Strawberry

○ Harmony Hammie

She never runs out of jokes, but she
might run out of good ones!

Personal Quote: Orange you glad to
see me?

Hides in: orange creamsicles

Bestie: Calista Creamsicle

○ Kitty Smitty

This kitty doesn't litter. She has a heart of gold.

Personal Quote: It never helps to
throw a hissy.
Hides in: chocolate strawberry
smoothies
Bestie: Selena Strawberry

○ Padma Panda

She's roly and poly with a
great big imagination!

Favorite Element: panda-monium
Personal Quote: Reach for the stars!
Hides in: cherry froyo
Bestie: Cherry Chica

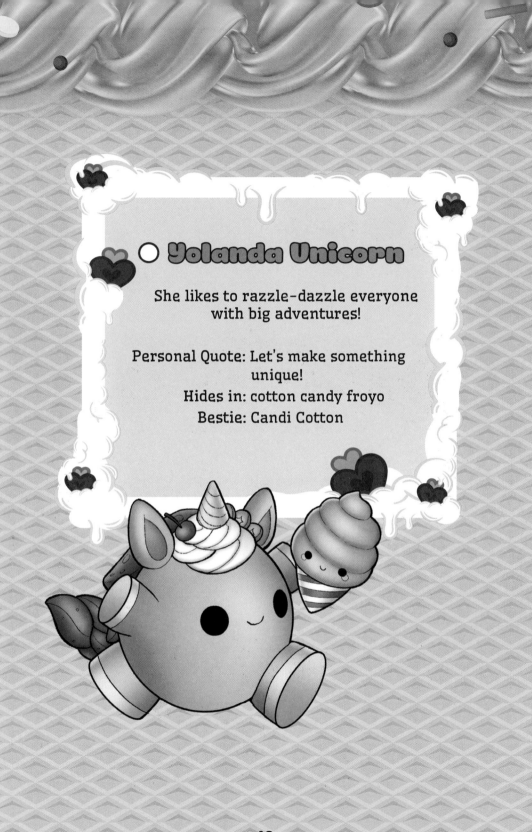

◯ Yolanda Unicorn

She likes to razzle-dazzle everyone
with big adventures!

Personal Quote: Let's make something
unique!
Hides in: cotton candy froyo
Bestie: Candi Cotton

⭘ Holly Husky

Always in a hurry, do-nut call
this pup late for dessert!

Personal Quote: What's shakin'?
Hides in: cookies 'n cream milkshakes
Bestie: Darla Dunkz

◯ Libby Llama

Llaugh all you want, this llama
is a serious kidder.

Personal Quote: Alpaca my bags!
Hides in: donut sprinkles shakes
Bestie: Candi Cottoncorn

◯ Nixie Narwhal

Don't be fooled by the blue, she's
always happy to see a friend!

Personal Quote: Have I got a whale of a
tale to tell you!
Hides in: cotton candy froyo
Bestie: Sheila Shake

RARE

○ Selma Sloth

She's a quick thinker, if not
so fast on her feet.

Personal Quote: Let's hang!
Hides in: cotton candy milkshakes
Bestie: Marsha Mallow

Play Sets!

● Harper Seal

She can't wait to chill with
your Smooshy friends!

Personal Quote: Come on in,
        the water's fine!
Hides in: the Collector's Fridge

⭕ Charlita Chicky

She can whip up a delicious breakfast,
even if she's winging it!

Personal Quote: Today's special is fresh-squeezed fun!
Hides in: Sunny Side Cafe
Bestie: Olli Orange

BENTOS

Discover which pets can only be found in bento boxes! Series 1-3

○ Gabby Gooey Raccoon

Mischief is her middle name. When opportunity knocks, she scurries to open the door.

Best Part of a Snack: the melty cheese, of course!
Treat: pizza
Besties: Pepper-O-Nee Pizza and
Raina Raspberry Macaron

○ Yummy Peppy Pup

His eyes are bigger than his stomach, but just barely!

Best Part of a Snack: a bun with a lot of bounce!
Treat: cheeseburger
Besties: Cailie Cake and Penelope Pickle

○ Sassy Fussy Fox

If only being sly were its own reward,
but this level of sneakiness deserves a treat!

Best Part of a Snack: sharing it with friends!

Treat: taco

Besties: Marlowe Avacado and
Chelsie Churro

○ Harper Hippo

She's a hippo, so she goes
and eats what she eats.

Best Part of a Snack: wearing it, so you always
have some for later!

Treat: cereal

Besties: Emma Eggie and
Wanda Waffle

Libby Labby

This proud pup knows her worth, and she deserves extra pickles!

Best Part of a Snack: Savoring every bite!
Treat: cheeseburger
Besties: Freddie Fries and Heather Heartsicle

○ Riley Red Panda

You would get tired of eating bamboo, too!

Best Part of a Snack: Slurping contests!
Treat: noodles
Besties: Dottie Dumpling and
Reena Rice Bowl

○ Heidi Hen

This early bird gets the pancake.

Best Part of a Snack: Sharing it at sunrise!
Treat: pancakes
Besties: Harley Hashbrown
and Jazmine Juice

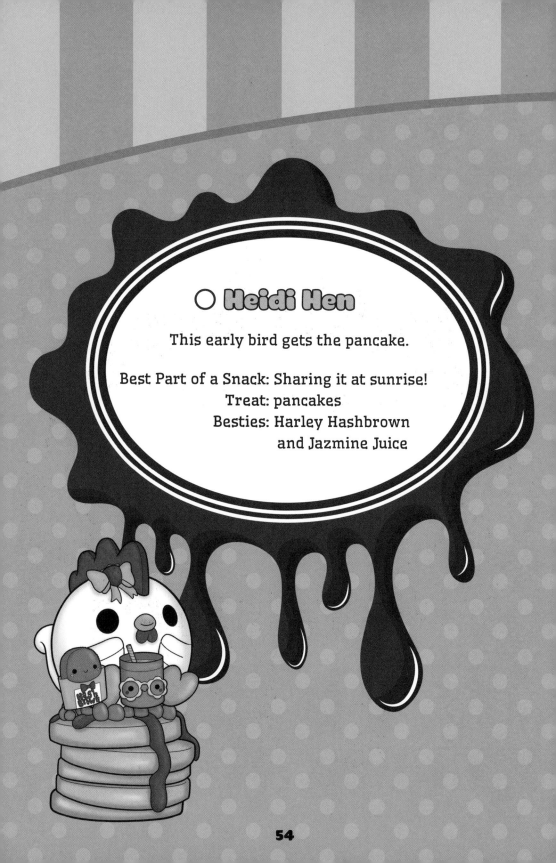

○ Benjamin Bulldog

Please, sir, may he have some more?

Best Part of a Snack: It's a po-ta-toss up!
Treat: fish and chips
Besties: Felix Fishstick and
Princess Penelopea

○ Lolli Lamb

Ewe can't blame her for trying!

Best Part of a Snack: Having good taste.
Treat: udon
Besties: Rita Riceball and
Sheila Sushi

Movie Munchies!

Ketchup, and mustard, and
3-D glasses, oh my!

○ Tillie Turtle

Usually the last to arrive, she's
quick to come out of her shell.

Personal Quote: Turtle-loo!
Hides in: ketchup bottle
Besties: Pippa Pretzel and
Henley Heartsicle

○ Pixie Pupcorn

When it comes to snacks,
she's a dog with a bone!

Best part of a snack: double features!
Treat: popcorn
Besties: Natalie Nachos
and Peta Pop

PUP CORN

Find Your Perfect Smooshy Pet!

Choose the answer that fits you best. Then, add up your points and find out which Smooshy Pet is your best match!

1. To go on an adventure, I need:

a. Encouragement
b. A plan
c. A buddy who's down for anything
d. Someone to hold me back

2. When I'm sad, I want someone to:

a. Tell me what to do
b. Cheer me up
c. Just listen
d. Pat me on the back

3. My dream vacation includes:

a. High-flying adventure like zip-lining
b. Swimming, hiking, or skiing
c. Walking around and exploring
d. Hanging out at a hotel

4. I'm happiest when I'm:

a. Trying something crazy
b. Trying something new
c. Laughing with my friends
d. Hanging out at home

5. Pick a color:

a. Red
b. Pink
c. Purple
d. Blue

6. On a team, I'm:

a. Someone you can count on
b. A great cheerleader
c. Easily distracted
d. Feeling super-shy

For each answer, give yourself the following points:

a = 1 point
b = 2 points
c = 3 points
d = 4 points

My Total Points: _____

22-24 points:

19-21 points:

16-18 points:

14-15 points:

12-13 points:

10-11 points:

8-9 points:

6-7 points:

My Perfect Smooshy Pet: _____

Bestie Collector's Checklist

Series 1: Bakies

- [ ] Bella Blueberry Macaron
- [ ] Reina Raspberry Donut
- [ ] Fifi Frosted Toast
- [ ] Suki Strawberry Cake

Series 1: Sweeties

- [ ] Chiya Cherry Popsicle
- [ ] Winnie Whip Cream
- [ ] Kandy Candy Apple
- [ ] Shyla Sugar Cube

Series 1: Munchies

- [ ] Drina Drumstick
- [ ] Olla Orange
- [ ] Joli Jelli Toast
- [ ] Shaya Sushi
- [ ] Samira Smore Super Rare

Series 2: Bakies

- [ ] Cocoa Muggins
- [ ] Piper Peanut
- [ ] Flo Fudgepop
- [ ] Sabina Sweet

Series 2: Sweeties

- [ ] Blinky Berry
- [ ] Caramel Crunchbite
- [ ] Bradley Bar
- [ ] Toasty Jamjar

Series 2: Munchies

- [ ] Charlie Churro
- [ ] Francois Franchum
- [ ] Emily Frostingcake
- [ ] Penelope Pastry
- [ ] Ramona Redpepper

Series 3: Snackies

- [ ] Casey Corndog
- [ ] Fortuna Cookie
- [ ] Nikki Nugget
- [ ] Rachel Ricetreat

Series 3: Sweeties

- [ ] Barry Berrymallow
- [ ] Mina Melon
- [ ] Penelope Pineapple
- [ ] Vee Nilla Creme

Series 3: Munchies

- [ ] Coco Creme
- [ ] Malory Fudgepop
- [ ] P.B. Jamison
- [ ] Poppy Kernels
- [ ] Teddy Taco *Super Rare*

Series 4: Snackies

- [ ] Bobbi Rito
- [ ] Peta Pop
- [ ] Sydney Siracha
- [ ] Teddi Spaghetti

Series 4: Sweeties

- [ ] Dippy Nana
- [ ] Hazle Spread
- [ ] Jully Gel
- [ ] Millie Milk

Series 4: Munchies

- [ ] Macarena Cheese
- [ ] Stella Stacks
- [ ] Tasha Take-Out
- [ ] Yolanda Yogurt
- [ ] Tanya Taiyaki   Super Rare

☐ Trixie Taffy

☐ Chloe Cotton Candy

☐ Tanner Twizzlestix

☐ Landon Lolli

☐ Petunia Pop

☐ Summer Berry Crunch

☐ Pia Peachring

☐ Trina Trufflet

☐ Cammie Crunch

☐ Gabi Gumball

☐ Aniston Applering

☐ Ryan Rock Candy

☐ Bobbi Bubbles

☐ Air Tina Taffy

☐ Air Lana Licorice

☐ Air Cassie Crunch

☐ Air Rae Rainbow

☐ Air Ryan Rock Candy

☐ Air Lexi Lolli

☐ Air Bobbi Bubbles

☐ Air Mallory Mallow

☐ Air Pia Peachring

☐ Air Sophie Sweetheart

☐ Air Aniston Applering

☐ Air Mary Mallow

☐ Air Lola Lolli

Movie Munchies

☐
Carmela Corn

☐
Lulu Licorice

☐
Casey Corndog